READY
FOR
PUMPKINS

Kate Duke

Alfred A. Knopf · New York

I am Hercules.

I live in Miss MacGuffey's first-grade classroom.

It's a good life.

The food pellets come regularly, the water bottle is always filled.

The first graders think I'm cute.

They like to teach me things.
They taught me how to paint.

And last fall I learned all about Halloween.
All in all, I thought I was a pretty lucky guinea pig.
I thought I had everything I could ever want.

Then spring came.

The children were busy—they planted
seeds in pots on the windowsill.

I was busy, too—taking naps in the sun.

One day I noticed that plants were growing in the
children's pots, and green beans were growing on the plants.
Real green beans!

Delicious!

All at once I wanted to be more than just a classroom
guinea pig. I wanted to grow things, too. I wanted a garden
of my own.

When school was over for the summer, I had my chance.

Miss MacGuffey brought me to my vacation home in the country.

When no one was looking, I put my plan into action.

Luckily, I had saved some Halloween pumpkin seeds.
Luckily, I knew what to do with door latches. Most
luckily of all, I found a friend to help me.
Her name was Daisy.

Daisy knows all about gardens. She showed me what to do. We found a sunny spot.

We pulled up all the weeds.

We dug up all the dirt.

Next we dropped each seed into its own hole and gave
it a drink of water.

At last the garden was ready. And I was ready, too—
ready for pumpkins!

But the seeds weren't ready.
Seeds can take a long time.

They don't grow faster if you yell at them.
    They don't grow faster if you jump up and down
and stamp your feet.

They won't grow at all if you dig them up to see
what they are doing.

I tried all these things. Finally Daisy said,
"Cool it!"

So I cooled it.
I tried to be patient.

I waited.
And waited
    and waited
        and waited.

Waiting is hard.
Daisy helped me do it.

She told me stories about famous pumpkins in literature.

Together we made up pumpkin poems and songs about seeds.

At last the seeds sprouted. Every day the little plants got bigger.

They grew leaf
    after leaf
        after leaf.

My seeds had turned into a garden!
The plants made buds.

The buds became flowers, and the flowers
turned into very small green pumpkins.
Amazing!
Daisy and I did a flower dance every time
it happened.

The pumpkins kept growing.

They were round and perfect—and they were mine.

Then birds and beetles came.

They pecked my pumpkins and ate holes in the leaves.

Worst of all, Daisy ate some of the pumpkin flowers.

MY pumpkin flowers!

I yelled. I jumped up and down.

I waved my arms and stamped my feet.

Finally Daisy said, "Cool it!"

So I cooled it.

The beetles ate some more holes, the birds kept pecking, and Daisy sometimes had a flower snack—but there was enough for all of us. Sometimes I had a flower snack, too.

A garden is not a place
to be angry in.

The pumpkins were still green when it was time to go back to school.

It was hard to say goodbye to them.

And hard to leave Daisy, too.

But you can't stay sad for long when you have had a garden.

And I had things that were just as good as pumpkins.
I had pumpkin poems and stories and songs.

I had flower dances to practice.
At night I could dream pumpkin dreams.

And I will have another garden next year.

I know where I can get some seeds.

Like I said, I'm a pretty lucky guinea pig.

To Sidney
—K. D.

THIS IS A BORZOI BOOK PUBLISHED BY ALFRED A. KNOPF

Text and illustrations copyright © 2012 by Kate Duke

All rights reserved. Published in the United States by Alfred A. Knopf,
an imprint of Random House Children's Books,
a division of Random House, Inc., New York.

Knopf, Borzoi Books, and the colophon are registered trademarks of Random House, Inc.

Visit us on the Web! randomhouse.com/kids

Educators and librarians, for a variety of teaching tools, visit us at
randomhouse.com/teachers

Library of Congress Cataloging-in-Publication Data is available upon request.

The illustrations in this book were created using watercolor and pen and ink.

MANUFACTURED IN CHINA
August 2012
10 9 8 7 6 5 4 3 2 1

First Edition